Jungle Journey

By Mara Conlon
Based on an episode by
Frank Rocco

SCHOLASTIC INC.

New York   Toronto   London   Auckland   Sydney
Mexico City   New Delhi   Hong Kong

ISBN: 978-0-545-19722-9

Based on the TV series *Wow! Wow! Wubbzy!* as seen on Nick Jr.®, created by Bob Boyle.

Published by Scholastic Inc. SCHOLASTIC and associated logos are trademarks and/or registered trademarks of Scholastic Inc.

12 11 10 9 8 7 6 5 4 3 2 1   10 11 12 13 14/0

Printed in the U.S.A.   40
First printing, January 2010

Daizy found a new pet at the park.
"I'm going to name you Princess!"
said Daizy.

"Hi, Wubbzy!" said Daizy.
"Do you want to play with Princess?"

"Sure!" Wubbzy said.

Wubbzy kicked the ball to Princess.

"Uh-oh!" said Wubbzy.
"Boop!" said Princess.

"Oh, no! Princess ran away!"
shouted Wubbzy.
"Lavender lollipops!" cried Daizy.
"She must have gotten scared.
We have to find her!"

"She's not under the slide,"
said Daizy.

"She's not in the mailbox,"
said Wubbzy.

"She's not in the bush!" said Daizy.

Wubbzy and Daizy looked in the pond.

But Princess was not there.
"Oh, Wubbzy!" said Daizy.
"How will we ever find Princess?"

Wubbzy had an idea.
They could ask Walden
and Widget to help.

"What kind of pet is it?" asked Walden.
"She has pink dots!" said Daizy.
"And a horn!" Wubbzy added.

"Princess is a unihorn!"
said Walden.
"Unihorns like the jungle.
The jungle has bugs,
marshes, and animals!"

"We have to bring Princess home!"
cried Daizy.
"To the jungle!" said Wubbzy.

"Watch out for doodlebugs!"
said Wubbzy.

"This marshmallow marsh is
sticky!" said Walden.

"Look at that chippy chipmunk!"
said Widget.

"Look!" said Walden.
"It's Unihorn Meadow!"

Unihorns were everywhere!

"Why do they keep saying *boop*?"
asked Wubbzy.
"*Boop* is the unihorn word
for *home*," said Walden.

"So this is Princess's real home?"
asked Daizy.
"Yes," said Walden.
"Now she is with her real family."

Daizy would miss Princess.
"We will visit you soon," said Daizy.
"Now we have to go back to *our* home."

"I think you mean . . . " said Wubbzy,
"it's time for us to go . . . *boop!*"